# Mysterious Miss Slade

# DICK KING-SMITH

# Mysterious Miss Slade

## ILLUSTRATED BY ANN KRONHEIMER

CROWN PUBLISHERS ★ NEW YORK

Text copyright © 1999 by Fox Busters, Ltd.
Illustrations copyright © 1999 by Ann Kronheimer
Jacket illustration copyright © 2000 by Roger Roth

Published by Crown Publishers, a Random House company, 1540 Broadway, New York, New York 10036. Originally published as *The Witch of Blackberry Bottom* in Great Britain by Viking Penguin Children's Books in 1999.

CROWN and colophon are trademarks of Random House, Inc.

www.randomhouse.com/kids

*Library of Congress Cataloging-in-Publication Data*
King-Smith, Dick.
[Witch of Blackberry Bottom]
Mysterious Miss Slade / Dick King-Smith ; illustrated by Ann Kronheimer.
—1st American ed.
p. cm.
Originally published as: The witch of Blackberry Bottom. Great Britain :
Viking Penguin Children's Books, 1999.
Summary: When eight-year-old Patsy and her younger brother befriend their old neighbor and her many animals, the children help the mysterious lady change her life.
[1. Helpfulness—Fiction. 2. Neighbors—Fiction. 3. Animals—Fiction.]
I. Kronheimer, Ann, ill. II. Title.
PZ7.K5893Mg      2000
[Fic]—dc21      99-046886

ISBN 0-517-80045-4 (trade)
ISBN 0-517-80046-2 (lib. bdg.)

Printed in the United States of America
June 2000

10  9  8  7  6  5  4  3  2  1
First American Edition

# CHAPTER ONE

THE FIRST THING you noticed was the smell.

Just outside the village there was a little turning, where quite a steep lane led down into a wooded hollow. This hollow was almost surrounded by trees, and as you went down the lane toward it, the smell hit you.

To people it was just a strong farmyard smell, of manure and muck, but to a dog, with his far more sensitive nose, it would have meant a whole host of things.

He would have detected the scent of a lot of other dogs, and cats and goats and chickens, and a faint whiff of donkey. There was a human being down there in the hollow, too, his nose would have told him.

If he had ventured nearer, he might have set eyes on her, and this is what he would have seen:

A very tall, thin woman, dressed in very old

clothes, some of which looked as though they had been made from sacks (which some of them had), surrounded by a pack of dogs of all shapes and sizes. On top of a mop of frizzy gray hair, she wore a man's flat cap, and beneath the cap was a quite unusual face, a strong brown Roman-nosed face, etched with deep lines. Under bold eyebrows, one very blue eye looked out upon the world. Over the other eye was a black patch.

No one in the village could remember how long Miss Slade had lived in Blackberry Bottom. It seemed as if she had always been there in her ancient caravan, surrounded by a cluster of old huts and sheds made of wood and tin, in which most of her animals were shut at night.

No one in the village much cared to go down the lane into that hollow, partly on account of the smell and partly because, over the years, the villagers had come to believe that Miss Slade was different from ordinary people.

"You keep away from there," they told their children, "if you know what's good for you. You keep well clear of that old woman down Blackberry Bottom."

"Why?" the children asked.

"Because she's a witch, that's why."

Not that the village children always obeyed. Some did, being frightened at the idea, but there were boys and girls who would make their way down the steep lane, moving cautiously, smelling that fruity smell, and hearing below them the barking of dogs, the meowing of cats, the bleating of goats, the cackle of chickens, and sometimes the creaking groan of a donkey.

The boldest might spy Miss Slade in her sack-like clothes and her flat cap, and perhaps

she might catch sight of them with her one good eye. If she did, she would wave an arm at them.

Actually, this was a beckoning gesture— "Come along, then, come and see me if you want to"—but to the children it seemed that she was signaling, "Get out of here! Clear off!" and even the boldest then turned tail and ran. After all, she was a witch; their parents had told them so.

It was a bit different if they met Miss Slade away from Blackberry Bottom, when, once a week, as a rule, she would pay a visit to the village shop to buy her groceries and other things.

On that day, a Wednesday usually, she would harness her donkey to a little wooden tub-cart that she herself had made from odd bits of wood and parts of scrapped cars. Then, leaving her dogs to look after the rest of the animals, she would drive up the steep lane to the village.

If she met other people on the way or in the shop, she would say to the grownups, "Good morning," and mostly, they would reply in the same way, though some just looked away. None actually held their noses, but the farmyard aroma surrounding Miss Slade was strong.

To children she would say, "Hello, and how are you today?"

Mostly, they would mumble, "All right," though some were struck dumb at the sight of the witch.

Everyone noticed how well-spoken she was, her voice cultured and pleasant.

"Talks so well as the Queen, she do," they said.

"Not short of money neither, is she?" they said, for Miss Slade's weekly shop was an expensive one.

On the return journey the little tub-cart was full of food for herself, and dog food and cat food and goat food and chicken food and always a bag of carrots for the donkey, so that he had to dig in his heels and brace himself against the weight as they descended the lane again.

One Wednesday evening, Miss Slade sat in her caravan, surrounded by her dogs and cats. Though old and rather battered, it was a large, roomy caravan, which was just as well, considering the number of those dogs and cats.

The six dogs were all mongrels, varying in size from one very large, mastiff-sized animal to one not much bigger than a guinea pig. From puppyhood they had all been trained to be nice to cats, though the cats (there were six of them,

too) treated the dogs with disdain, considering themselves to be a higher class of animal.

Later that night the cats would be put out of the caravan to roam about Blackberry Bottom, and the dogs would be shut in one of the sheds, except the smallest, who spent her nights on Miss Slade's bed as a hot-water bottle.

The goats had their shed, the chickens theirs, and the donkey slept in his own special house, which had been the body of a baker's van and still had

JOHN JENKINS, BAKERS
FRESH BREAD DELIVERED DAILY

painted on its outside.

Miss Slade had no electricity in her caravan, so it was by the light of an oil lamp that she now addressed her audience of dogs and cats.

"Another day's shopping over and done with, my dears," she said. "And I hope you've all had enough to eat."

The cats, as usual, did not respond to this speech. They merely stared at her glassily, but the dogs wagged their tails at the sound of her voice, and some flattened their ears in pleasure, and the smallest one gave a string of little yaps. She did this each evening, and Miss Slade liked to think that what she was saying, speaking for all of them, was: "Tell us about your day."

"Well," said Miss Slade, "my day was much as usual, except that I met more children than normal, it being the school holiday, but I regret to have to tell you that when I asked them how they were, none of them said anything in reply except 'All right.' Now, as you all know, I have never had a child of my own (though of course I think of you all as my little family). But I do like children, and I often think how nice it would be if some of them—even just one or two—sometimes came down here to Blackberry Bottom and talked to me. I should so enjoy that."

She sighed.

"I wonder," she said, "if they ever will?"

# CHAPTER TWO

ON THE SIDE of the hill above Blackberry Bottom stood a cottage, where two very old people had lived for a long, long time. The prevailing wind in those parts was westerly, and the cottage was to the west of Miss Slade's domain, so that the old people seldom noticed the smell; nor, both being rather deaf, were they bothered by the noise of the various animals.

But then one day the old man died, and his wife, with nothing much left to live for, soon lay beside him in the churchyard. So the cottage came up for sale.

It was bought by a young couple who had two children, a girl of eight called Patsy and a boy of six called Jim. None of them, of course, had ever heard of Miss Slade, let alone the story that she was a witch.

The day after they moved in, the children

walked down across the fields from their new home while their parents were unpacking and came into the steep lane that descended into the hollow.

They also came upon the smell.

Jim held his nose.

"Blimey!" he said. "What a stink!"

Patsy sniffed.

"It's manure, I think," she said.

"What's manure?" asked Jim.

To both children, everything about the countryside was novel. They had been born and brought up in a town and knew nothing much about life in the country.

"Manure," said Patsy, "is dung."

"What's dung?" asked Jim.

"Well, it's what animals do, like cows. You know what a cow pat is, don't you?"

They had walked on down as they were talking, so that soon they came to the bottom of the hollow and saw in front of them the caravan and the huts and sheds (with a lot of hens scratching and pecking about among them) inside a sort of fence. A very rough fence it was, built, of course, by Miss Slade herself out of all sorts of things, most of which she had dragged home from the local dump—wooden panels, sheets of corrugated iron, old headboards—

all of them kept together with assorted bits of old wire.

There was a kind of gate in this fence, made out of an old door fixed on its side, just wide enough to allow the tub-cart in and out. As a fence to keep animals in, it was quite useless, for the hens could flutter over it, the cats climb over it, and the goats and the dogs (except the smallest) jump over it. Really, it seemed only to keep the donkey from getting out, which he did not want to do anyway: apart from Wednesdays, when he had to pull the cart, he was quite happy to stay inside Miss Slade's property, eating the thistles and nettles and other weeds that grew everywhere.

Now the children stopped abruptly at the sight of no less than six dogs that suddenly appeared, all barking—one, a huge one, in a very deep voice, and one, a tiny one, in a very shrill yap.

Jim grabbed Patsy's hand.

"Let's go home," he said.

But at that moment they heard a loud voice that cried, "Be quiet, the lot of you!" and the dogs fell silent. Then out of the caravan stepped the tall figure of an old woman, dressed in shapeless clothes and wearing a man's flat cap on top of her mop of frizzy gray hair and a black patch over one eye.

She looked across and saw the two children standing at the foot of the lane and waved an arm at them.

When, unlike other village children, they did not move, she said to the six dogs, "Sit!" and they all sat. Then she came forward to the fence and pulled the makeshift gate open.

"Hello," she said in her pleasant voice, "and how are you today?"

"Let's go home," said Jim again, tugging at his sister's hand.

But Patsy, looking at the strange figure before her, decided that she was not frightened. You shouldn't talk to strangers, she knew, but this one spoke so nicely and had such a nice smile that she answered, quite naturally, "We're very well, thank you."

"I'm extremely glad to hear it," said Miss Slade. "Although I have to confess that I don't recognize either of you. Is this the first time you've come down here?"

"Yes," said Patsy. "We've just moved in, to the cottage on the hill, yesterday."

Only yesterday, thought Miss Slade, I was

saying how nice it would be if some children, even just one or two, came down here and talked to me. And today—here they are, like magic. How extraordinary. Anyone would think I was a witch.

"I must introduce myself," she said. "My name is Miss Slade, and this place is called Blackberry Bottom, and these are some of my friends."

She turned to the row of sitting dogs and called, "Edward!" and the largest, mastiff-sized one got up and lumbered over to the children, tail wagging slowly. His great wrinkled face was level with Jim's.

Perhaps you shouldn't pet strange dogs, Patsy thought, but this one looks very friendly. So she did, and after a little while, so did her brother. Then Miss Slade called up four more dogs, one after another. Muffin was a sort of hairy cow dog, and Marmalade was smooth, more like a greyhound, and there were two smaller, terrier-like ones called Nip and Tuck.

Finally, when each one of these had been introduced in turn, Miss Slade summoned the very small, guinea pig–sized, yappy little dog, whose name was Tiddler.

"There!" she said. "Now you know all of us.
So what are *your* names?"

"I'm Patsy," said Patsy, "and this is my
brother, Jim."

"How do you do?" said Miss Slade, and she
shook hands with each in turn.

Jim looked up at her.

"Are you a pirate?" he said. "Pirates have
black patches like that."

"No, actually, I'm not," said Miss Slade. "It's
just that I've only got one good eye. I lost the
other one."

"Couldn't you find it again?" asked Jim.

Miss Slade laughed.

"It was an accident," she said. "A long, long time ago, when I was about Patsy's age. One Guy Fawkes Night. Always remember, both of you, to be terribly careful with fireworks. Now then, come in and meet my other friends."

Patsy and Jim's parents had never kept an animal of any sort, not even a cat. Now the children found themselves petting six cats, all of different colors; picking up, each of them, a warm brown egg that had just that moment dropped out of a hen; and drinking, each of them, warm, creamy white milk straight from a goat—to say nothing of having a ride, each of them, on a donkey.

The donkey, Miss Slade told them, was called Moke.

"Why Moke?" asked Patsy.

"It's just another name for a donkey."

"Is he old?" asked Jim.

"Yes, he's lived for a very long time. For donkey's years, as they say."

"Why do they say that?" asked Patsy.

"Because people say you never see a dead donkey."

"You will, when this one dies," said Jim.

"Oh, I think he'll probably outlive me."

"How old are you, then?" said Jim.

"I'm in my seventieth year," said Miss Slade. "That means I shall be seventy next birthday."

"I shall be seven," said Jim.

"Lucky old you," said Miss Slade.

At that moment they heard voices in the distance. There was a man's voice that sounded angry and a woman's voice that sounded agitated.

"Patsy! Jim! Where are you?" called the children's father and mother from the cottage on the hill above.

"We'd better go," said Patsy, and she yelled back, "Coming!"

"Thank you for everything," she said to Miss Slade. "I like all your animals, especially Edward."

"So do I," said Jim. "Specially Moke."

"Come again," said Miss Slade. "I've much enjoyed meeting you both."

"I like her, too," said Jim to his sister as they ran off up the lane. "Even if she does smell, it's a nice smell."

# CHAPTER THREE

"WHERE ON EARTH have you been?" said the children's parents.

"We just went for a walk," said Patsy.

"Where to?"

"To Blackberry Bottom," said Jim.

"What? Where's that?"

"Down there," said Patsy, pointing. "We talked to ever such a nice farmer."

"I don't care how nice he was," said her father. "You know quite well we've told you not to speak to strange men."

"She's not a man, she's a woman," said Patsy.

"A strange woman," said Jim.

"She's got lots of animals," said Patsy.

"I should think she has," said her mother, "judging by the state you're both in. Your clothes are filthy. What have you got all over you?"

"Manure, I expect," said Jim. "She's got lots of manure, Miss Slade has."

"Now, you listen to me, both of you," their father said. "You keep away from this Miss Slade person, d'you hear me? You are not to go down to this Blackberry Bottom place again, d'you understand?"

That night Patsy and Jim lay in bed in their new rooms feeling quite sad at the thought of not being able to see Miss Slade and her animals again.

Especially the big dog, Edward, thought Patsy.

Specially Moke, thought Jim.

In the caravan down below the cottage, Miss Slade lay awake, feeling happy.

"Patsy and Jim!" she said out loud. "Such nice children, don't you think, Tiddler?" But the smallest dog, snuggled up against her feet in the musty warmth at the bottom of the bed, did not answer.

Outside, Edward and Muffin and Marmalade and Nip and Tuck and the goats and the chickens slept in their various sheds and huts, and old Moke dozed in the body of the baker's van, while through the night, silent save for the cry of owls, the six cats stalked.

I hope they'll come again soon, was Miss

Slade's final thought before sleep overtook her.

But they didn't. Not the next day, not for a week, not for a month, and though Miss Slade looked about for them on her Wednesday shopping trips, she did not see them, because, of course, they were now at the village school.

Their very first day, the older children found out that Patsy lived up above Blackberry Bottom. They lost no time in warning her.

"There's a horrible old woman lives down there," they said. "Dirty smelly old thing. A witch, she is. Don't you go near her—none of us ever have."

Poor Miss Slade, thought Patsy, but she said only, "Our dad won't let us go down there."

"He's right," they said. "Specially with Halloween coming up next Saturday. She'll come up out of there, flying on her broomstick."

Jim, of course, was with the younger children, and after school Patsy asked him, "Did anyone say anything to you about Miss Slade?"

"No," said Jim. "Why should they?"

"Well, in my class they were saying she's a witch."

"Blimey! Is she?" said Jim. "Wow!"

"No, of course she isn't; she's too nice. I nearly said that to them because they were saying nasty things about her, but I didn't."

"Why not?"

"I don't know, I suppose I wasn't brave enough. I suppose I thought that if they knew we'd made friends with her, they'd start saying nasty things about us. Let's not tell them we've been in Blackberry Bottom with her."

"All right," said Jim, "but I wish we could go there again."

"We can't. You know what Dad said."

As it turned out, the schoolchildren had been partly right, because at Halloween the next Saturday, Miss Slade did come up out of Blackberry Bottom—not on a broomstick but on Moke.

Though tall, she was not heavy, and the donkey carried her happily enough up the steep lane out of the hollow. She met no one, for not even the boldest of the village children would have dared come that way on that particular night.

Once on the road, Miss Slade turned up another, more gentle lane that led to the old cottage on the hill above. She steered her steed one-handed with an old rope halter. On the other arm she carried a basket. The great dog Edward walked beside her.

Earlier, she had held her usual conversation with her dogs. She did this each day after she had fed them, filling the six feeding bowls, which ranged in size from Edward's enormous dish to Tiddler's tiny one.

She sat down facing them, and as usual, Tiddler gave her string of little yaps.

"Well, my dears," she said to them, "this evening I am going to pay a visit to our new neighbors. Something tells me that the reason why Patsy and Jim have not come back to see

me is because their parents have forbidden them to. I don't know why. What do they imagine I am—a witch? Come to think of it, it's Halloween! So you'd better come with me, Edward, to protect me from any witches we might meet on the way. The rest of you can stay here in the caravan till we get back."

She patted the coarse gray blankets under which she slept.

"Jump up here, you others," she said, "and warm the bed ready for me."

It was quite dark by the time Miss Slade reached the cottage on the hill, but she could see

by the light streaming out its windows that there was a large brass knocker on the front door. She rode Moke right up to the door, turned him sideways, and reached for the knocker.

Inside, Patsy and Jim's mother said, "Someone at the door."

"Whoever could that be?" said her husband.

"Children, I expect," she replied. "Trick or treat."

"Eh?"

"It's Halloween, you know."

"Oh, so it is. But I can't believe any of the village children would be bothered to come all the way up here after dark," said Patsy and Jim's father. He laughed. "More likely it's a witch!" he said. "Flown up here on her broomstick."

He could hardly have been more surprised if it had been when he did open the door.

Standing just outside, in the light from the opened door, was a donkey on whose back sat the strangest figure and by whose side stood a massive dog. His immediate thought, when he saw this ragged-looking old woman with a black patch over one eye and a man's flat cap on her gray hair, was that this must be a gypsy, come to sell clothespins or sprigs of lucky heather.

But before he could speak, the woman said in the pleasantest of voices, "Please forgive me if I'm wrong, but do Patsy and Jim live here?" and then the children pushed past him, crying, "It's Miss Slade! Hello, Miss Slade!" Patsy put a hand on Edward's great head, and Jim patted Moke's gray neck.

"My question is answered," said Miss Slade to their father, and to their mother, who had now appeared in the doorway, she said, "I must apologize for disturbing you, but I had the great pleasure of meeting your children some weeks ago, since which time I have not seen them again."

"We couldn't come," said Jim.

"I hope you've not been ill?"

"No," said Jim, "but Dad said…"

"Be quiet, Jim," said his father and his mother and his sister with one voice.

Miss Slade smiled.

"I quite understand," she said.

Seeing that pleasant smile and hearing that pleasant voice, the children's father suddenly felt extremely uncomfortable. This old woman— old *lady*, I should say, he thought—suspected, perhaps somehow knew, that he had forbidden any further visit to her.

"I'm sorry, Miss, er, Slade," he said. "We should have introduced ourselves. I'm Robert Reader and this is my wife, Susan."

We can't very well ask her in, he thought, what with the dog and the donkey, and anyway, she doesn't look all that clean. In fact, to be honest, she looks rather like a witch.

"Is there something we can do for you?" he asked.

"No, no, thank you very much," said Miss Slade. "I merely came to introduce myself as, I think, your nearest neighbor, and to bring you a small present." And she handed down to Susan Reader the basket she was carrying. In it were a dozen brown eggs.

"New-laid," said Miss Slade.

"How very kind of you," said the children's mother. "Let me just go and put them in a bowl, and then you can have your basket back."

"Oh, don't bother with that," said Miss Slade. "I daresay Patsy and Jim can return it to me, one of these days?" And she smiled at both the adults and winked at both the children by closing her one good eye. Then she turned Moke's head and spoke to Edward, and off they went into the night.

# CHAPTER FOUR

AT BREAKFAST THE next day, Sunday, November the first, the Reader family were all eating boiled eggs—lovely, big brown new-laid eggs—when Patsy said, "We'd better take Miss Slade's basket back, hadn't we?"

"She might need it," said Jim.

Their father looked at them quizzically.

"No hurry, is there?" he said.

"Don't tease them, Bobby," his wife said. "You can see what they're after, can't you?"

"Look, Sue," said the children's father. "I've told them. They are not to go down to this Blackberry Bottom place on their own."

He went on eating his egg as though the subject was closed.

"We wouldn't be on our own," said Patsy, "if you and Mum came, too."

"It's a very nice morning for a walk," said Jim.

So it was that after breakfast they set off down the gentle lane from the cottage, turned onto the road, and turned off again down the steep lane that led to the hollow.

As before, the smell came up to greet them.

"Oh!" said the children's mother.

"Ugh!" said their father.

"It's only manure," Patsy said.

"Dung!" said Jim. He sniffed appreciatively. "I'm getting to like it," he said.

As they approached the fence, the dogs appeared, barking, but fell silent again at the sound of Miss Slade's voice, coming from inside one of the tumbledown huts.

"Quiet!" she shouted, and then called, "I shan't be a moment, whoever you are. Just finishing milking." And in a little while the door of the hut opened and out she came.

She was carrying a bucket full of milk and was followed by several goats, who made off through a crowd of foraging hens, leaped easily over the fence, and disappeared among the trees.

"Good morning!" called Miss Slade, coming toward the gate. "How nice to see you all again so soon."

"We've brought your basket back," said Patsy.

"How good of you. And on All Saints' Day, too. Which must mean that you are all saints. Do come in, won't you?"

Patsy and Jim's mother and father shot hasty looks around.

"It's very kind of you," they said. "But we can't stay."

How can she live in such a place? they thought. Muck and mess and rubbish everywhere.

"We've an awful lot to do at home," they said.

"Still getting the house straight."

"And the garden, of course."

"It'll be quite some time before we get everything tidy."

Miss Slade laughed.

"'Tidy,'" she said, "is, I'm afraid, a word that I have somehow forgotten. I really must make an effort and get rid of some of my rubbish."

"It's Guy Fawkes Day on Thursday," said Patsy. "You could have a bonfire."

"We could bring some fireworks," said Jim.

Instinctively, Miss Slade raised a hand to touch the black patch that covered her sightless eye.

"Kind of you, Jim," she said, "but I'm not

keen on fireworks, you know. Anyway, they would frighten my animals very much. But you have given me an idea."

"What?" said the children.

"Well, most of the rubbish that, I'm afraid, you can see around here is composed of odd bits of wood. Now then, Mr. and Mrs. Reader, if you were thinking of having a bonfire for the children up at your cottage this Thursday, you'd be welcome to all this old wood."

"It's nice of you, Miss Slade," they said, "but we really don't have the time to collect it."

"But I do," said Miss Slade. "I've got all the time in the world. I could load it onto my tub-cart and Moke could pull it up the hill to you. You'd be doing me a favor."

At these last words the Readers hesitated. We can hardly refuse, each thought. Robert Reader looked around at the litter of battered planks and posts and pallets and broken boxes and smashed crates and even the wreck of a wooden hut that had collapsed and died of old age.

"But it will take you ages to load up all this stuff," he said.

Miss Slade smiled.

"Not if I had Patsy and Jim to help me," she

said. "I bet we could clear it out today."

The Readers looked at one another.

"I shall quite understand if you say no," said Miss Slade. "But we should be killing two birds with one stone. I'd be getting rid of some of my rubbish, and you'd get the materials for a really whopping bonfire. You don't know me, of course, but I can assure you that I like children and that yours will be perfectly safe with me, today or any day. Please say they can help."

"Oh, can we?" cried Patsy and Jim. "Please?"

Their parents looked at the eager young faces and then at the brown, lined, black-patched old face that was smiling down at them. And each

thought that though this person might not often, if ever, apply soap and water to that face or comb that hair or change those dreadful clothes, she was, without doubt, both honest and kind.

"Well, if you're sure they won't be in the way…" they said.

"They'll be the greatest help," said Miss Slade. "And don't bother about their midday meal. We'll do one load this morning, and then we'll have lunch in my caravan and do a second load this afternoon. I don't cook, I'm afraid, because I have no electricity, but I do buy myself a lot of things that they might like, such as chips and cookies and cakes and chocolate and Coca-Cola."

"All right, this *is* a special occasion…" the Readers said, looking again at the three excited faces.

"Yummy!" said Patsy.

"Wow!" said Jim.

When the children's parents had set off back up the lane, Miss Slade said, "Now, the first thing to do is to harness Moke to the tub-cart. He usually pulls it only on a Wednesday, when I do my shopping, so he might be a bit awkward about having to work on a Sunday."

But in fact, whether it was the novelty of

having the children stroking and patting and talking to him or whether it was the extra-large carrots that Miss Slade produced for them to give him, Moke behaved perfectly, and soon they were ready to load the cart with wood.

"Watch out for nails," said Miss Slade, "and mind you don't get splinters in your hands, and leave the heavy bits to me."

When the tub-cart was piled high with wood, she tied down the load with some old rope, and they were ready to set off.

"Now then, Tiddler," Miss Slade said, "into the caravan you go, and the rest of you, you stay here and look after the place, understand?"

"Can't Edward come with us?" said Patsy.

"All right, if you like."

So off they went—Miss Slade walking on one side of the donkey, holding his bridle, and Jim walking on the other, and Patsy and Edward walking behind the cart—till they came to the steepest part of the lane, where they (except Edward) got behind and pushed to help Moke.

When they reached the cottage on the hill, the children's father helped them unload the wood, and they piled it at the bottom of the garden. Then they (including Edward) got into

the tub-cart and drove back down again to have
their picnic lunch in the caravan.

While they were eating, Patsy asked Miss
Slade how she managed without any plumbing
or electricity.

"I have an oil lamp," she said. "But I go to bed
very early, and then I get up as soon as it's light.
That time of day is the best of all, especially in
spring and summer."

"How d'you keep warm in the winter?" Patsy
asked.

"Lots and lots of blankets, and Tiddler on my
feet for a hot-water bottle."

"What about drinking water?"

"I buy spring water for myself and the dogs,

and there's a pond where the other animals drink."

Patsy was going to say, How about washing? but then she didn't, for it was plain that Miss Slade didn't wash much, if ever.

Jim paused in the middle of his second bag of sour cream and onion potato chips.

"How do you manage about"— he swallowed his mouthful—"going to the...you know?" he said.

"A lavatory, d'you mean?" asked Miss Slade.

"Yes."

"I go to Jericho," she said.

"Where's that?"

"I've got an outhouse—'Jericho' is an old

name for it." She pointed out of the window, and there, between the caravan and the next shed, which belonged to the goats, was a very small, narrow building the size and shape of a telephone booth.

"Wow!" said Jim.

"Some people call them thunder boxes," said Miss Slade, at which Jim began to snigger and then Patsy started to giggle and then Miss Slade joined in, till the three of them were laughing like lunatics.

As it grew dark on the evening of All Saints' Day, Miss Slade stood alone on the step outside her caravan—alone, that is, apart from her animals—thinking what fun the day had been.

In the early afternoon they had driven a second load up to the cottage, and now, looking around in the dusk, she could see that the place really did look a little bit tidier.

She remembered the expressions on the faces of Mr. and Mrs. Reader that morning when they had first set eyes on her property. Horrified, they had been!

I suppose I have let things slide a bit, she said to herself. Perhaps I ought to make a bit of

an effort, now that I've got these nice new neighbors. Buy some new sheds perhaps, maybe even a new caravan. After all, it's not as though I couldn't afford it.

The villagers were right when they said to each other that Miss Slade was not short of money. She had lots of it, in cash—notes and coins of many kinds, including even a store of gold sovereigns.

Everyone loves stories about hidden treasure.

No one knew that for a great many years now, there had been a wealth of treasure hidden right under their noses.

In Blackberry Bottom.

# CHAPTER FIVE

NO ONE KNEW anything much about the strange old woman who lived in Blackberry Bottom—except her name.

No one had the faintest idea that she was, in fact, an aristocrat, the only daughter of the late sixth Baron Culpepper of Culpepper Castle, and that her full and proper name was the Honorable Margaretta Slade, born to a life of riches and luxury and brought up in the stateliest of homes, waited upon by a host of servants.

As a child she had wanted for nothing until that other Guy Fawkes Day, more than sixty years ago now, when the loss of an eye had altered her life.

It was not simply the accident that changed things, for she grew into a tall, handsome girl, and the black patch she always wore lent her a rakish, piratical look that many found attractive.

But one young man did not, and he, alas, was the one with whom, in her early twenties, she was to fall deeply in love. For a while, perhaps because of the rank and wealth of her family, he led her to think that he loved her in return. But then he decided he would prefer a wife with two good eyes and married someone else.

This was the start of the descent of the Honorable Margaretta Slade from the heights of Culpepper Castle to plain Miss Slade in the depths of Blackberry Bottom.

For there are people who love once and then never again, and she was one of those. First had come the loss of an eye and then, partly because of that, a broken heart, for she never got over the loss of the man to whom she had given that heart.

Gradually, she dropped out of the circle of rich, well-born young people with whom she had led a carefree, pleasure-filled life and began to lead a solitary existence, turning her back on the world.

Because, as a child, she had always had everything done for her—by her nanny and later by her own lady's maid—she had never learned to take care of herself in any way. She did not know how to make a cup of tea, how to boil an egg, how to sew on a button, how to wash as much as a handkerchief. Everything had always been done for her.

Now, living alone, she had to do all these things for herself, and at first she made some effort to look after herself. But then came another tragedy, when both her father and her mother were killed in an airplane crash.

A cousin inherited the title and Culpepper Castle, but all Lord Culpepper's considerable wealth, including his prized collection of gold sovereigns, was left to the Honorable Margaretta.

At first Miss Slade kept her fortune in the bank, drawing money when she needed it, living alone meanwhile in rented apartments or hotel rooms. But as time went by, she gradually changed, taking less and less care of herself and growing scruffier with each passing year. Then she began to move about the country from place to place, looking for a plot of land to buy where she could live and where there was room to keep the animals that she had always loved from childhood. She liked walking and did a great deal of it, and one day by chance she walked down a steep lane into a hollow and found there, surrounded by trees, a rough field with a pond in one corner.

Immediately, she knew that this was where she wanted to live. She bought it, and then she bought a large caravan and a number of sheds and huts and had them installed there.

Then she began to collect the animals she wanted.

By the time the Readers came to live in the cottage on the hill, Miss Slade had been in Blackberry Bottom so long that no one could remember a time when she hadn't been there.

And as time passed, so the caravan and the sheds and the huts and Miss Slade grew older and scruffier. But she still had lots of money, far more than she would ever be able to use, however long she lived. And she kept it in Blackberry Bottom.

When she had first bought the plot there, those many years ago, she had decided she wanted nothing more to do with banks. Visiting the bank to get money meant a journey into the nearest town. Why be bothered with that? She would keep it close by. But where?

And then Miss Slade had an idea that appealed to her sense of humor. At one side of

the field she had bought, behind the spot where the caravan was now parked, was a grassy bank. In the top of it she dug a deep hole, just the right size to hold an old ten-gallon milk churn standing upright. Into the hole she fitted the churn.

Then she arranged with her bank manager to have all her money ready, in notes plus the hoard of gold sovereigns, and she collected it one day, going into town by taxi with two empty suitcases and coming out with them full. Back at Blackberry Bottom, she carried in the suitcase full of treasury notes, leaving the taxi driver to bring in the one filled with her late father's collection of coins.

"Stone the crows, miss!" he said. "What you got in here—bricks?"

"No," said Miss Slade. "Gold sovereigns."

"Oh, pull the other one, miss," said the taxi driver. "You don't expect me to believe that!"

Miss Slade laughed.

"No," she said. "I don't."

She's crazy, she is, said the driver to himself as he drove away. Gold sovereigns, indeed! Why, there ain't such things anymore.

Later that very night—a bright moonlit night it was—Miss Slade dropped the money into the ten-gallon milk churn that was buried in the grassy bank behind the caravan with only its lid showing. Then she covered over the lid with earth and leaves and branches.

"Now," she said, "if anyone asks me where I keep my money, I'll tell them: I keep it in my bank!"

From then on, all Miss Slade had to do each Wednesday morning was to walk a few paces from the caravan, brush away the earth and leaves and branches that hid the lid of the churn, take the lid off, reach down into the churn, and collect whatever money she wanted. Then she covered it back up again.

And so it had gone on for years and years and years, and still there was lots of money left in the milk churn.

Miss Slade's last thoughts on that All Saints' Day, as she lay in bed—fully dressed, as usual—with Tiddler on her feet, were that on Wednesday, the day before Guy Fawkes Day, she could buy fireworks for Patsy and Jim. I shan't, of course, she said to herself, but their father will, and I'm sure he'll be very careful. What nice people they are, Robert and Susan. I wonder if someday I may be allowed to call them that. It's ages since I had any friends.

Oddly enough, that Wednesday morning she met Susan coming out of the village shop.

"Oh, good morning, Mrs. Reader," she said.

"Good morning, Miss Slade," said the children's mother. "And please, won't you call me Susan?"

"I should like that," said Miss Slade. "On condition that you call me Maggie. The real name with which my parents saddled me is Margaretta, which I've always disliked. I see you've been buying some fireworks for Patsy and Jim."

"Yes," said Susan, "and I'm glad to have met you. I was going to walk down to Blackberry Bottom to ask if you'd like to come up to us tomorrow evening when we set these off, before we set light to your enormous bonfire."

"Nice of you," said Miss Slade, "but in fact, I'm not too keen on fireworks."

She put up a hand and tapped her black patch.

"Did the children not tell you?" she asked.

"No," said Susan. "You mean..."

"Yes, when I was a child."

"Oh, I'm so sorry," said Susan Reader.

She paused, not knowing quite what to say next.

Then she said, "We'll meet again soon, I hope."

54

"I shall look forward to that," said Miss Slade. She smiled. "Good-bye, Susan," she said, holding out her grimy, roughened hand.

Patsy and Jim's mother took it in her soft, clean one, smiling also.

"Good-bye, Maggie," she said.

# CHAPTER SIX

As SHE WATCHED her husband setting off the children's fireworks the following evening, Susan Reader found herself thinking of the old lady below the hill.

Later, when the bonfire was well alight and they all four stood around it, listening to the crackling of the blazing wood and the roar of the flames, their faces lit by the glare, she said, "That's how she lost an eye, did you know?"

"What?" said her husband. "Who?"

"Miss Slade. It was a fireworks accident, when she was a little girl. I met her yesterday in the village and she told me, after I'd asked her if she'd like to come tonight."

"Poor old girl," said Robert Reader.

"I feel awfully sorry for her," Susan said.

"Because she lost an eye long ago?"

"Yes, that, of course, but mostly because she's

let herself get in such a state. I mean, she's a lady, you can hear it in her voice, and yet she lives in that filth—like a dirty old tramp."

"She's probably happiest like that," her husband said.

"I don't think she is. I think she's lonely and friendless."

"She's got two friends, at least," said Robert, looking at Patsy and Jim as they stood together, gazing entranced into the heart of the fire. "They keep asking when we can go down to Blackberry Bottom again."

The children's mother was silent for a moment. Then she said, "I wish we could help, Bobby."

"Help? Who?"

"Maggie."

"Who's Maggie?"

"Miss Slade."

"Oh, we're on first-name terms, are we? Look, Sue, I know you. Your heart's as soft as putty. Next thing, you'll be asking her up to lunch or supper. Can you imagine? I mean, let's be honest, she actually smells! I shouldn't be surprised if she never takes those clothes off—sleeps in them, probably."

"I know," his wife said. "But there's something awfully nice about her."

She looked down the hill.

"I wonder if she can see the bonfire," she said.

In fact, Miss Slade had been in her caravan having her evening chat with the dogs when she heard the first crack of a rocket from the hill up above.

"You stay in here, my dears," she said. She went outside and stood looking up and saw another rocket burst in a shower of golden globes, and then several more. She thought of the children, not just these ones here but children everywhere, enjoying the sights and sounds of this one special night.

Without thinking she put her hands together, as she had been taught to do long ago, by her nanny, at bedtime.

Please, she thought, let no one be hurt, especially Patsy and Jim.

She stood there till the few fireworks were over and the hill above Blackberry Bottom was once more in total darkness. Because of the surrounding trees, she could not see the lights of the Readers' cottage, but soon she saw, above

the treetops, a golden glow that lit the sky, and knew that the bonfire was burning.

The Readers are burning up just a little bit of my rubbish, she thought, and she remembered how clean Susan's hand had been yesterday, and her young, unlined face and her clothes and her hair. I suppose I should be surprised she could bring herself to shake hands with me, she thought. There's no real chance of becoming a friend of the Readers'. And why not? she asked herself. Because you're a mess, Maggie Slade, that's what you are. You live in all this filth, like

a dirty old tramp, and it's only now, now that you've met this family, now that you've had some kind words from them, that you have finally realized it.

She went back inside the caravan.

"Do you realize," she said to the six dogs, "that in a few weeks' time it will be my birthday, and that then I shall have lived the full biblical three score years and ten?"

Six tails—three long and three stumpy— wagged as the dogs sat looking at her.

"I have to tell you," she said to them all,

"that beginning on my seventieth birthday, I am going to turn over a new leaf." And something in her voice, some note of determination, made Tiddler let out a volley of shrill, excited yaps.

# CHAPTER SEVEN

SUSAN READER WAS not, by nature, someone inclined to mind other people's business. But she did feel that if she was to be of some help to Miss Slade, she must somehow find out more about her. She did not quite want to invite her up to Partridge's (as the cottage on the hill was called, after the old couple who had lived there so long). Why don't I? she asked herself. Because, she replied, to be honest, I don't want her tramping into the house in her mucky old Wellies or sitting on my newly covered chairs in those dreadful old clothes.

Who would know anything about her? she was asking herself on the morning of the following Wednesday.

Her husband had left for work, taking the children in the car with him to drop them off at school, and she was clearing away the breakfast things when the mailman knocked at the door.

"Tell me," she said to him when she had taken the letters, "what is the proper address of my neighbor, Miss Slade? You must deliver her letters, too."

"Address?" said the mailman. "Oh, just Blackberry Bottom. There's only one such place and only one Miss Slade. She'm a bit touched, you know, not quite right in the head. I don't know if you've ever been down there, but it's a proper dump. She don't hardly ever get any mail, but when she do, I just sticks them in her

letter box, if you can call it a letter box—it's an old cookie tin wired onto her fence."

"Perhaps she can't afford anything better," Susan said.

"Not afford it?" said the mailman. "She's got plenty of money, she has. Wednesdays, she spends a fortune at the village shop. I should know — 'tis my cousin as runs it. She'll be in there this morning, buying food for herself and her animals; she's not short of a few quid, I tell you. Pity she doesn't spend a bit on herself, buy herself some decent clothes instead of going about in those old rags."

By a strange chance there was, among the mail that the mailman had delivered, a brightly colored illustrated catalog from a company selling mail-order clothes. Susan Reader, about to throw it away, suddenly thought: Miss Slade. She leafed through it, noting that the clothing, though expensive, looked to be of good quality. It was principally hard-wearing outdoor stuff such as might be worn by wealthy country people. And Maggie Slade, she said to herself, is apparently a wealthy countrywoman. I'll walk down to Blackberry Bottom and stick it in her letter box while she's out shopping. And she took a felt-tip marker and blacked out her own address. You never know, she thought, something in it might catch her eye.

So she waited till mid-morning—when, judging by the time of their meeting last week, Miss Slade would be out—and then set off. But when she reached the top of the steep lane leading down into the hollow, she found she had left a bit late. Coming along the road from the village was the tub-cart.

Miss Slade pulled Moke to a halt.

"Susan!" she said. "Were you looking for me?"

Shall I? Shan't I? thought Susan. The last

thing I want to do is hurt her feelings...oh, come on, let's go for it!

"Yes, Maggie, I was," she said. "This came in the mail this morning, and I thought perhaps you might like to have a look through it. It's one of these direct-order catalogs. You just ring them up and they mail you the clothes."

"Kind of you," Miss Slade said, "but I haven't bought any clothes for years."

But then I *did* say I was going to turn over a new leaf, didn't I? she thought.

The *reason* I thought of you, said Susan to herself, is precisely *because* you haven't bought any clothes for years.

"The reason I thought of you," she said to Miss Slade, "is that I noticed these jackets"— and she opened the catalog at the right page, which she had dog-eared—"and I told myself that they would be exactly the thing for you, out in all winds and weathers as you often are."

Miss Slade looked.

FIRST FROST, FIRST SNOW WON'T FAZE
OUR COZY TEFLON-COATED FIELD JACKETS

it said, and there was a brightly colored photo-

graph of five of these jackets: one khaki, one brown, one green, one navy, and one (which was "Women's only") a bright red.

"The red one's nice, don't you think?" said Susan.

"Sixty-seven pounds fifty!" said Miss Slade. "It's not cheap, is it?"

But you can afford it, thought Susan. If the mailman's right, you can afford to buy a whole lot of new clothes.

But I can afford it, thought Miss Slade. For a seventieth birthday present to myself, I can afford to buy a whole lot of new clothes.

She dropped Moke's reins so as to have both hands free to flick through the catalog.

"Heavens!" she said. "I've never seen one of these things before. How colorful the clothes are. And so sensible, too. Look, Susan—'Winterlochen Tunics.' And 'Contour-Fit Leggings.' And 'Fisherman's Rib' sweaters."

She turned the pages, murmuring, "Gloves," "Scarves," "A hat with earflaps."

"A very good selection of clothes they have, it appears to me," she said, and she made to hand the catalog back.

"No, no, you keep it, Maggie," said Susan. "I don't want it. And if you should like anything, you can order by telephone."

"I don't have a telephone," said Miss Slade.

"No, but I do. Anyway, I'll just leave it with you. I must be getting back now."

That evening Miss Slade sat in her caravan with the six dogs, as usual, and told them—after Tiddler had yapped at her to do so—about meeting Susan Reader and being given the mail-order catalog. She opened it at the dog-eared page and showed them, by the light of the oil lamp, the picture of the Teflon-Coated Field Jackets. She pointed to the red one.

"I've rather fallen in love with that one," she said. "I think I might buy it. I told you—didn't I?—that I'm going to turn over a new leaf."

She turned the pages of the catalog.

"And perhaps this…" she said, "and this… and this. D'you know, my dears, I'm beginning to feel quite excited about it all. I suppose it's high time I made a bit of an effort to smarten myself up. For donkey's years now, I've been looking like a dog's breakfast."

# CHAPTER EIGHT

AT BREAKFAST THE next day, Jim said, "Dad, are we poor?"

"Well, no," his father replied. "I wouldn't say that."

"Well, are we rich?"

"No, we're not rich."

"Well, what, then?" said Jim.

"We're quite comfortably off," his mother said. "Daddy's got a good job at the bank, so we don't have to worry too much about money. Why are you asking, Jim?"

"Well, our teacher was telling us about Robin Hood and how he and his merry men robbed the rich people to feed the poor ones."

"I hope your teacher also told you," said his father, "that robbing people is not a good idea, however rich they are. And anyway, I bet Robin Hood didn't give anything to the poor, he just pocketed it all."

"But, Dad," said Patsy, "don't you think we ought to help poor people? Like Miss Slade, I mean. She must be very poor."

"Why do you say that?"

"Because her clothes are so old. Even if we're not rich, couldn't we give her some money to buy new ones?"

"No."

"Why not?" said Patsy. "The vicar came to Assembly the other day, and he was saying that Jesus said, 'Sell all you have and give it to the poor.'"

"We ought to give Miss Slade something," said Jim. "She gave us those eggs."

"Why don't you draw a picture for her, Jim?" said Susan. "You're good at drawing. She'd like that."

"And I could do a poem for her," said Patsy.

"Yes, that'd be nice."

"And then," said Patsy, "we could take them down to Blackberry Bottom and give them to her. On Saturday, perhaps?"

"All right. I'll walk down with you," said her mother, thinking of the catalog she had given Miss Slade. I don't suppose she'll buy anything, she thought.

So on Saturday morning, Robert Reader went off to play golf, as usual, and Susan and the two children walked down to Blackberry Bottom together. At the barking of the dogs, Miss Slade appeared at the door of her caravan.

"Hello!" she shouted. "Come in, come in. Don't mind the dogs—they won't hurt you."

"I've brought you a present," said Jim, and he handed her a large scroll of paper.

"How lovely!" said Miss Slade, and she unrolled it and smoothed it out.

It was a picture of an animal, she could see—

a four-legged animal of some sort—standing in some very bright green grass under a very bright blue sky, out of which shone a very bright orange sun. What kind of animal it was might have been a mystery to Miss Slade had not Jim written MOKE in very bright red letters under the picture.

"Jim," said Miss Slade. "That is beautiful. I shall pin it up on the caravan wall."

"And I've brought you a poem," said Patsy, and she held out a sheet of paper.

Miss Slade read it.

*Blackberry Bottom is cool and shady*
*And there lives a special lady*
*With her dogs and goats and hens and cats*
*And the cats kill lots and lots of rats*
*And she has a donkey that pulls a cart*
*And it's easier to make him stop than start*
*And the special lady is our friend*
*And she is called Miss Slade.*

*The End*

"Patsy," said Miss Slade, "I don't think anyone has ever written me a poem before, and even if they had, this would be much the nicest." And she pulled out a handkerchief that

had once been white and with it dabbed her eye.
She sniffed.

"Oh, Susan," she said, "what lovely children
you have. And how glad I am to see you, because
I was going to come up to ask you a favor."

"Please do, Maggie," said the children's
mother.

Miss Slade produced the catalog.

"I have decided," she said, "to buy myself
some new clothes."

"Oh," said Susan. "Oh, good."

"Mostly warm things. For the winter," said
Miss Slade. "And now that I've made my mind

up, I'd quite like to order them. You can order by phone, it says, and I wondered if you'd be kind enough to order for me."

"Of course I will, Maggie."

"The other thing is—I don't bother with credit cards or checkbooks, so could you pay for the whole lot if I give you the money in cash?"

"Certainly."

"Now, I've made a list of all the things I want and added them up, including the postage. It comes to three hundred and fifty-five pounds, and I've got it all ready somewhere—where did I put it?—oh, yes, in this empty cornflakes box." And she counted five twenty-pound notes, twenty ten-pound notes, and eleven five-pound notes, while the children goggled at the sight of so much money.

"Goodness, Maggie!" said Susan Reader. "Look, it's none of my business, but I mean, should you be keeping such large sums of cash here? Suppose someone stole it while you were out?"

"Like Robin Hood," said Jim.

"You probably don't know," Susan went on, "but Robert is a bank manager. I'm sure he could open an account for you if you wished."

76

"Don't worry, Susan," said Miss Slade. She smiled. "I have my own bank," she said.

The mailman was right, Susan thought as they walked back up to Partridge's. She's not short of a few quid.

# CHAPTER NINE

THE FOLLOWING WEDNESDAY, Miss Slade came out of her caravan early and climbed up on top of her grassy bank to get money for shopping. As usual, she scraped away the earth and leaves that concealed the metal lid, took it off, and reached an arm down into the milk churn.

She pulled up some notes and some coins and dropped them into an old leather satchel with a shoulder strap. As usual, she didn't look to see how much she'd gotten out. If she'd taken too much, then on her return from the shop, she'd simply put back what she hadn't needed.

Because of their weight, the gold sovereigns lay at the bottom of the churn, so there wasn't much risk of picking one of them out by mistake. But this day by chance she did.

Chance was to play an even bigger part in things that morning, for as Miss Slade was

reaching into her satchel in the village shop to pay for her purchases, she just happened to drop a coin on the floor, and that coin just happened to be the one gold sovereign. Moreover, Susan Reader just happened to be coming toward the shop as Miss Slade was driving away in the tub-cart, and when she went in, she just happened to catch sight of the gold coin lying in a corner.

Susan bent and picked it up. The shopkeeper was serving someone else, and Susan was about to say, "Look what I've found. D'you know who it could belong to?" when something told her quite definitely that it was Miss Slade's, that Miss Slade must have dropped it.

I'll keep it for her until I see her next, she said to herself, and she popped the sovereign into her pocket.

That evening, after the children had gone to bed, she showed the coin to her husband.

"Look, Bobby," she said. "You know what this is, I'm sure."

"Good Lord," said Robert. "It's a gold sovereign. Where on earth did you get that?"

So she told him.

"It must belong to Maggie," she said. "She must have money hidden away somewhere."

"But why would she do that, Sue?" said Robert. "I thought she told you she had her own bank."

"She did."

"Which one? She doesn't bank with me."

"I don't know."

"Well, obviously you're going to return this sovereign to her. Maybe you'll find out more about the buried treasure of Blackberry Bottom."

Susan fingered the gold coin.

"What's one of these things worth nowadays, Bobby, d'you know?" she said.

"A heck of a lot, I should imagine. I can find out. What's the date on that one?"

"1922."

On Thursday morning, Susan was about to set off for Blackberry Bottom when Robert phoned to say that he'd found out the value of a gold sovereign.

"You'd better tell Miss Slade," he said.

As Susan walked down the steep lane to the hollow, she heard the strangest noise below. Partly it sounded like someone singing, partly it sounded like a lot of dogs howling. It was both.

"O come, all ye faithful!" sang Miss Slade loudly as she swept out her chicken house. "Joyful and triumphant!" But though there may have been something triumphant in her singing,

there was nothing joyful about it for the six dogs. They sat in a row outside the chicken house and howled dolefully at the sound of their mistress's voice.

"Hello, Susan," said Miss Slade when the hubbub had died down. "It's always the same. I always start singing carols about this time of year, but it always sets the dogs off. They just don't appreciate the beauty of my voice. What can I do for you, Susan?"

"Oh, nothing, thanks, Maggie," Susan said. "It's just that I came into the village shop yesterday not long after you'd left—I saw you driving away—and I found this on the floor." She held out the sovereign. "I wondered if you'd dropped it?"

"Must have," said Miss Slade. "I didn't know I'd picked it out, but it's sure to be mine. My father used to collect them, as a sort of hobby, and he left them to me. I've got thousands of the things."

"Where do you keep them?" asked Susan.

"In the bank."

"Oh, good. Because they must be very valuable now," Susan said. She paused and then she went on, "In fact, I know they are. You'll have to try to forgive me, Maggie, for being nosy, but I showed this coin to Robert, and he rang me up just now to say that a sovereign of this date — or any sovereign between 1900 and when they stopped minting them — is worth about seventy-five pounds."

"Good gracious," said Miss Slade.

"And he also said that he'd found out that sovereigns were first minted in 1817, and that the older ones are worth much, much more."

"More than seventy-five pounds each?"

"Oh, yes. Some perhaps ten times that."

"Gosh!" said Miss Slade. "I've got lots of older ones, I seem to remember. Perhaps I'd better get them valued. Only I don't quite know how to go about it."

"Well, I'm certain Robert could help," Susan said. "As I told you, he is a bank manager, and I'm sure he could get in touch with the manager of your bank."

The Honorable Margaretta Slade shook her head slowly, smiling all the while.

"Susan," she said, "I think the time has come to tell you the truth. I've not known you that long, but long enough to trust you. And I think your husband could be a great help to me. As I've told my dogs, I'm going to turn over a new leaf. So—can you keep a secret?"

"Yes," said Susan Reader. "I can."

"Right," said Miss Slade.

She pointed behind the caravan.

"You see that grassy bank there?" she said.

"Yes."

"That is my bank."

"I don't understand."

"Come on," said Miss Slade. "I'll show you."

They climbed up on top together, and with

the broom that she had been using to sweep out the chicken house, Miss Slade swept aside the earth and leaves and twigs to reveal the metal lid of the milk churn. She took it off.

"Put your arm in, Susan," she said. "Go on, have a lucky dip."

Susan reached down into the churn and pulled out a fistful of treasury notes. Her bank! she thought. All her money, buried in a milk churn!

"Stick those back," said Miss Slade, "and reach down further."

Underneath the paper money, Susan could feel, was a solid mass of coins. She pulled up a handful. Some were the familiar coins of today, but three of them were gold sovereigns; and one of those, she could see, looking carefully at it, was dated 1850, nearly a hundred and fifty years old. Heaven knows what that one's worth! she thought.

Speechless, she held it out. Miss Slade took it.

"Hmm," she said. "Didn't know I had any that old."

Susan found her voice at last.

"Maggie!" she said. "Please, you *must* put this money somewhere safe. Anybody could come down here and find it."

87

"Oh, it's safe enough," said Miss Slade. "Anyway, apart from you and your family now, nobody much ever does come down here."

When the money had been dropped back into the churn, including the sovereign that Susan had found on the floor of the shop, and the lid had been put back on and camouflaged, both women turned to come down from the top of the bank. They were just too late to see the solitary figure that had been standing at the foot of the lane, watching them.

He had disappeared among the trees.

# CHAPTER TEN

A COUPLE OF days later, a Saturday, Miss Slade was looking at a calendar that hung on the caravan wall, next to Jim's work of art. Normally, she scarcely bothered about what date it was, and since her involvement with the Reader family, she had more than usually lost track of time. But now she saw that her birthday, her seventieth birthday, was approaching.

"And that's when I'm going to turn over a new leaf," she said to the dogs. "I told you, didn't I?" And Tiddler yapped. "But that means smartening myself up in the new clothes I've ordered, from knickers to noddle. But they haven't arrived! Oh dear, I did rather fancy being all dolled up for my birthday. If only I were a magician—a witch, let's say—I could make them arrive by saying a magic spell, something like...let's see, now..."

*What, no new clothes? Oh, what a worry!*
*Because I need you in a hurry.*
*You must no longer stay away*
*But come to me this very day!*

And then the dogs barked, and Miss Slade, looking out of the little window of the caravan, saw a car draw up by her gate and the whole Reader family get out. The parents were each carrying a huge parcel and the children each a smaller one.

"Your mail order's arrived, Maggie!" called Susan.

"Oh, how wonderful!" cried Miss Slade, and she opened the door of the caravan in an excited hurry and rushed out toward the gate. Not looking where she was going, she caught her foot in an old coil of wire and fell, hitting her head against the gate with a bang the Readers all heard.

Dropping their parcels, they ran forward, to find Miss Slade lying unconscious while the dogs sniffed anxiously at her.

Robert Reader pushed through them and knelt beside her.

"Is she all right?" the others asked.

"I think so," he said. "But she's knocked herself out cold. We'd better get her to the Cottage Hospital. Give me a hand with her, Sue."

The dogs sat watching silently (even Tiddler) as their mistress was lifted gently into the car.

"I'll drive," said Robert. "You sit and hold her, Sue. And, Patsy and Jim, you go straight home and wait for us to come back, understand? We shan't be long. The front door key is inside the old green watering can, as usual."

"Wait, Bobby," said Sue. "We'd better put these parcels back in the trunk. She's going to

need a lot of stuff out of them, because I know what the hospital will do with the clothes she's got on."

"Burn 'em?"

"Yes."

"She's not going to die, is she?" said Jim as he and his sister walked up the steep lane in the wake of the departing car.

"No, of course not, she only hit her head," said Patsy.

"She's old, though," said Jim. "You get weaker as you get older. Perhaps she's bust it."

"Don't be silly," said Patsy.

"Hope she hasn't," said Jim.

Near the top of the lane they met a man coming down. He had a bushy gray beard and was dressed in very ragged clothes.

"It's a tramp!" said Patsy to Jim in a low voice.

"Are they fierce?" said Jim a little shakily.

"No, of course not, but don't speak to him."

"Hello there!" said the tramp as they met. "Have you young 'uns bin visiting the old lady as lives down there?"

"Yes," said Patsy, "but she's not there. She's gone to the hospital."

"You said, 'Don't speak to him,'" hissed Jim.

"Oh, you can speak to me, all right," said the tramp. "I'm a relation of hers, you see. Hospital, eh? I better go on down to see what I can do to help."

"Are you Miss Slade's brother?" asked Jim.

"Brother? Oh, yes, yes, I am," said the tramp, and he hurried on.

"I thought he was," said Jim. "They look ever so alike."

"I don't believe a word of it," said Patsy. "He doesn't talk anything like Miss Slade. She speaks like a lady. I bet he's going to try and pinch something. Let's watch and see."

So they turned off the lane and made their way back through the trees and hid behind some bushes on the rim of the hollow. They saw the tramp go through the open gate, at which the dogs rushed up, barking. Whereupon he put his hand into the filthy pocket of his filthy overcoat and drew out what must have been food of some sort, for the barking stopped and all the tails, of varying lengths, began to wag.

Luring them on with the bait—stale bread, it was—the tramp opened the door of one of the sheds, threw the food in, and then, as they went for it, shut them inside.

Patsy and Jim saw him pick up an old pitchfork that was propped against the side of the
caravan and climb the grassy bank behind it.
He began to scratch about with the pitchfork,
scattering earth and leaves and twigs, in an
effort, it seemed, to find something. Along the
crest of the bank he went, prodding and poking
and peering, until suddenly there was a clang as
the tines of the pitchfork struck something else
made of metal.

Hastily, the tramp knelt down.

"What's he doing?" said Jim.

"It looks as if he's taking the lid off something," said Patsy.

And then they saw the man reach down with
one hand—reach down into the ground, it
seemed.

When he pulled it back out, the children
could see quite clearly from their hiding place
that clenched in his dirty fist was a great wad of
banknotes.

# CHAPTER ELEVEN

BY THE TIME the Readers reached the Cottage Hospital, Miss Slade had regained consciousness. At first she was a bit confused, but then, when they'd explained to her what had happened, all she wanted was to be taken back to Blackberry Bottom.

"When someone has had a proper look at you," said Robert Reader firmly, "and not before. Susan will stay with you while I dash off back and collect the kids."

In the emergency room, the other patients looked askance at the strange old lady who had been brought in, and after a while a nurse came around the waiting room, spraying it with an air freshener labeled SPRING VIOLETS.

Eventually, a young doctor examined Miss Slade and then took Susan Reader aside.

"Your...er...mother?" he said.

"No, no, just a friend," said Susan. "My

husband and I were with her when she fell and hit her head."

"Well, I don't think you have to be too worried," said the doctor. "There's no sign of concussion, so we shan't need to admit her. I don't think there's much wrong with her state of health—though, if you'll forgive me, her state of dress is, shall we say, less than clean?"

"Yes, I know," said Susan. "She's a recluse, you see, lives alone in an old caravan and keeps lots of animals."

"Caravan, eh? No washing facilities?"

"No," said Susan.

She looked at the doctor. "She…um… smells a bit, doesn't she?"

He grinned.

"Definitely," he said.

"Do you think," said Susan, "that before you discharge her, she could have a really good bath, here?"

"She can," said the doctor, "but after that, what she really needs is a complete set of new clothes. No good getting clean and then putting on those old rags again."

"That," said Susan, "can be arranged." And she told the doctor about the mail order.

"We brought the stuff with us," she said. "It's in Reception."

"Splendid!" said the doctor. "Tell me, are you a close friend of Miss Slade's?"

"I've not known her long," said Susan, "but I don't think she has any other friends apart from us. If you're thinking what I think you're thinking, regarding the clothes she's wearing now — yes, burn 'em!"

Back at Blackberry Bottom, Patsy and Jim watched in amazement as the tramp pulled more and more money out of the ground, stuffing it into his pockets in such a hurry that a puff of wind caught some of the banknotes and sent them fluttering everywhere.

"Look!" said Jim. "Look at all that money!"

"I told you," said Patsy. "He's a thief. He's pinching Miss Slade's money. She must have had it hidden there. We must stop him somehow."

"He'll beat us up," said Jim.

"Not if we have Edward and the other dogs to protect us," said Patsy. "Come on, quick, we must run down and let them out."

So busy was the tramp, jamming more and more money into every pocket he had, that he

did not notice the children making their cautious but hasty way down to the shed where the dogs were shut. At first, when Patsy opened the door, they made little noise, accustomed as they now were to the sight and scent of the children, but then they noticed the strange figure on top of the bank behind the caravan.

Urged on by the children, they all ran toward the tramp, barking loudly—Muffin and Marmalade, the two fastest, in the lead, followed by Nip and Tuck and Tiddler, with Edward lumbering behind.

If the tramp had kept his head, he might have gotten away with his booty. As it was, the sight of the whole pack of dogs rushing at him, excited by the cries of the two children he had met in the lane, was too much for him, and he slid down the grassy bank and made off.

For a moment it looked to Patsy and Jim as if the tramp *would* get away. He was running, shouting angrily and kicking out at the dogs, while Muffin and Marmalade circled giddily around him, and Nip and Tuck and a madly yapping Tiddler snapped at his heels.

But then the matter was settled as Edward caught up with them. Charging into the man, he knocked him over.

This was the scene that met Robert Reader's eyes as he drove hastily down the steep lane. He had hurried to Partridge's only to find the house still locked, with no sign of the children, so he had anxiously driven back to Blackberry Bottom. There, just inside the gate of Miss Slade's enclosure, he saw a ragged man with a bushy gray beard whose pockets were stuffed with what anyone, let alone a bank manager, could see was paper money. He lay flat on his back, for the simple reason that the great dog Edward was standing upon him, forepaws on his chest. Around them ran a frenzied circle of shouting children and barking dogs. In the background, unmoved by the rumpus, three goats stood calmly eating five-pound notes.

# CHAPTER TWELVE

"GET 'IM OFF me, guv'nor!" gasped the tramp as the children's father approached. "Get 'im off, he weighs a ton, honest!"

"Honest," said Robert Reader, "is one thing that you are not, by the look of you, my friend. Just where did you get all this money?"

"He stole it, Dad!" shouted Patsy and Jim. "We saw him!"

"Out of the caravan?"

"No, it was in a hole in the ground. On top of that bank over there. It's Miss Slade's money!"

"I'll give it all back, guv'nor!" cried the tramp. "Just get this thing off me chest!"

"Now, you listen to me," said Robert. "I'm making a citizen's arrest—d'you understand? I'll get the dog off, but then you stay right where you are. Don't try anything—I'm much younger

103

than you and a lot bigger, too. What's this dog called, Patsy?"

"Edward," said Patsy. "Come on, Edward, off you get, there's a good boy." And off Edward got.

"Go and find a sack," their father said to the children, and when they came back with one, he went through all the pockets of the supine tramp and dropped the money in.

"Now," he said, "I'll give you a choice. Either I hand you over to the police, or you give me your word that you will take yourself off, right out of this district, now."

"I will, I will, guv'nor, I swears it on me mother's grave," said the tramp.

"Get up, then," said Robert Reader, "and if you ever show your face round here again, I'll have the law on you, quick as a flash."

Empty-pocketed now, the tramp got to his feet. Edward growled deep in his throat, and the other dogs began to stir excitedly. But Patsy said, "Sit!" in a voice as nearly like Miss Slade's as she could manage, and they all sat.

When the tramp had hastily disappeared up the steep lane, the children took their father up onto the grassy bank behind the caravan. As they went, they all picked up five-pound, ten-pound, and even twenty-pound notes that the wind had blown around, while the disappointed goats watched.

Staring into the depths of the milk churn, the bank manager sighed deeply. What a way to keep your money, he thought. It's not earning a penny of interest. Well, it can't stay here, whether the old lady comes out of the hospital or not. Even if the tramp doesn't come back, anyone else might stumble on it. The only sensible thing is for us to collect it all.

He knelt down and began to pull out more

handfuls of banknotes. Soon the first sack was full, and the children went to find another one.

As he took out the last treasury note, their father could see that the lower part of the churn contained a solid stack of coins, including a huge number of gold sovereigns. Some of them, he saw, glancing at their dates, were old enough to be extremely valuable. She has a king's ransom in here, he thought.

At last the milk churn was empty, and they loaded the bags of money into the car.

"Jump in," said the children's father. "We must hurry now and fetch Mum from the hospital."

"And Miss Slade," they said.

"I don't know about that. They may keep her in."

"Well, if they do," said Patsy, "what about the animals?"

"We'll have to feed them," said Jim. "I get to feed Moke!"

"But who's going to milk the goats?" said Patsy.

"Me," said Jim. "It's easy. I've seen Miss Slade do it. You just squeeze 'em and the milk comes out."

I do hope that she is well enough to come home, thought Robert Reader as they drove away, or I can see us spending all our time in Blackberry Bottom.

At the Cottage Hospital, he was about to get out of the car when he realized that he could not possibly leave it unguarded, with a fortune in cash sitting in the trunk. So he sent the children in with instructions to ask for their mother.

He sat watching the main doors, wondering how to explain to an old lady still presumably shocked by her recent experience that all her money—apart from however many pounds' worth in the goats' stomachs—was in the trunk of his car.

In a while he saw his family coming out, accompanied by an unknown woman, dressed mainly in bright red.

On her feet were red boots, above them red leggings, and over a green fisherman's sweater she wore a brilliant red field jacket. All these clothes were obviously brand-new. As were the red gloves, the green scarf, and, on her head, the red hat with earflaps.

Who on earth...? thought Robert, and then he saw the black patch over the eye.

"Miss Slade!" he gasped.

"I wish you would call me Maggie," she said. "Susan does."

"Can *we*?" said Jim.

"Certainly not," said Susan.

"We could call you Auntie Maggie, couldn't we?" asked Patsy.

"I should be delighted if you did," said Miss Slade.

"But tell me, how *are* you, Miss...er... Maggie?" said the children's father.

"Fit as a fiddle, thank you, Robert. Luckily, I've got a thick skull. Tell me, how do you like my new clothes?"

"You look marvelous," said Robert.

And so clean, he thought. Her face, her hair—what he could see of it under the red hat with earflaps—her hands, her fingernails even, all looked beautifully clean.

"I feel like a million dollars," said Miss Slade.

"Talking of money," said Robert, "I must tell you—"

"I know!" said Miss Slade. "The children have just been telling me about the tramp and how dear Edward stood upon him. I should have liked to see that."

"If I may say so," said Robert, "it wasn't very wise to keep it where it was."

"I know," said Miss Slade. "It was just my silly joke. You know, 'My money's in my bank.' But I'm not too old to learn a lesson. So please, Robert, will you keep it in *your* bank from now on?"

Back at Blackberry Bottom, Miss Slade took off her lovely new red boots and pulled on a pair of filthy old Wellies.

"Goodness!" she said. "I've done no work at all today yet. I must start mucking out."

"Don't you think you should take things easy?" Robert said. "You have had a nasty fall."

"And you'll get your new clothes dirty, Auntie Maggie," said Patsy.

"Possibly," said Miss Slade, "but it'll be some time before they're *really* dirty."

"What'll you do then, Auntie Maggie?" said Jim.

"Buy some new ones, I expect," said Miss Slade. "If your father thinks I can afford them. I think I've just about got enough money, haven't I, Robert?"

# CHAPTER THIRTEEN

THAT AFTERNOON ROBERT Reader drove to the bank of which he was the manager, let himself in, and put into the vaults the two old sacks that contained Miss Slade's worldly wealth.

On the following Monday, he arranged for a taxi to pick her up from Blackberry Bottom and bring her in to his bank. (On *her* bank, a number of beetles had fallen into the now-lidless milk churn.)

When Robert came home that evening, he said to his wife, "I bet you didn't know something about your friend Maggie."

"My friend? *Our* friend, I should hope," she said.

"Okay, *our* friend Maggie. She is, actually, I find, the Honorable Margaretta Slade, only daughter of the late sixth Baron Culpepper of Culpepper Castle."

"Blimey!" said Susan. "Is that how she has that money?"

"It appears to be," said Robert. "She was left all her father's money and his unique collection of gold sovereigns. They, I should guess, will be worth a small fortune. I'm getting them valued for her. However you look at it, Maggie Slade is a very rich woman."

"Oh, Bobby, is she going to go on living in that awful old caravan among those awful old huts and sheds? It was so nice to see her so clean and tidy, and smelling of soap instead of muck. Can't you persuade her to buy a nice house?"

"No," said Robert Reader. "She is quite determined to stay in Blackberry Bottom, partly because she loves the place and partly, she said, because of us. Which I thought rather touching. But as to her lifestyle, she's going to change things. We discussed this at length, and the upshot is that she is going to buy a large modern caravan—one of those mobile-home things—that will have electric light and hot water and a shower and a bathroom and a cooker and a fridge and so on."

"And what about her animals?"

"She's going to buy new huts and sheds for them, and pay someone to get the place thoroughly cleaned up."

"What persuaded her to do all this, d'you suppose?" Susan asked.

"You, partly, I think," said her husband. "It all started with that mail-order catalog you gave her. I think she realized just how far she'd let herself go. And, of course, she's grown very fond of Patsy and Jim, she said."

The children, who had been watching television, came into the room—as children do—just in time to hear their names.

"Who's fond of us?" they said.

"Miss Slade."

"Auntie Maggie, you mean," they said.

"Anyway," their father went on, "she tells me that she's been planning to turn over a new leaf by a certain date."

"What date?" said Susan.

"December the twelfth."

"Why then?"

"It's her seventieth birthday. I didn't like to think of her being on her own down in all that mess and muddle, so I said we'd like to give her a birthday party, here at Partridge's. I hope I did right, Sue? At lunchtime, so she can get home before it's dark."

"You did quite right."

"Can Edward come?" said Patsy.

"And Moke?" said Jim.

"Can we have chips?" said Patsy. "Auntie Maggie likes them."

"And she likes chocolate cookies," said Jim, "and Swiss roll and Coke."

"*You* like them, you mean," said their mother. "The first thing I must think about is making a birthday cake."

"With seventy candles?" said Robert.

"No, I think I'll just write seventy on it in icing and then stick one candle in the middle of the zero."

As it turned out, the twelfth was as perfect a December day as you could wish: dry, no wind, not too cold, quite sunny even. Long before the appointed time, the children were on the look-out for their guest.

"She's coming!" they shouted at last, and the whole family stood at the front door of Partridge's to welcome the Honorable Margaretta Slade, who stood upright in the tub-cart dressed in her new clothes, the reins in one hand, waving with the other, that familiar black patch over one eye.

Tall and proud and straight-backed, she looked like a queen in her chariot. Beside her in the tub-cart stood great Edward, tail beginning to wag at the sight of the big marrow bone Patsy had ready. Even plodding old Moke quickened his step a little as Jim waved a bag of carrots.

Leaving dog and donkey to have their meal outside, the others sat down around the loaded table. In the center was the birthday cake, its one candle now lit.

"Oh, Susan!" said Miss Slade. "Did you make that?"

Susan nodded.

"How lovely! I haven't had a proper birthday cake since…oh, I don't know…since I was a child. And how thoughtful not to make me blow out three score and ten candles."

"Blow out that one now, Maggie," said Robert, and she did, and they all sang "Happy Birthday."

Looking slyly at Miss Slade's new clothes as they ate, Susan was pleased to see that as yet, they were not very dirty, though they did look rather as though they had been slept in (which they had).

And after they had finished eating—Susan and Robert a modest amount, Miss Slade a lot, and Patsy and Jim a great lot—they went to sit around the fire while the children went out and came back with a package.

"It's for you, Auntie Maggie," said Patsy, "from all of us."

"We gave some of our pocket money," said Jim.

"How very good of you," said Miss Slade.

"Yes," said Jim. "It was. I had to give fifty pence. It was a jolly expensive present."

After a lot of thought, Robert and Susan Reader had decided to buy Miss Slade a camera.

"She could take 'before' and 'after' pictures with it," Robert had said. "Blackberry Bottom as it is now, and then as it will be later."

"Oh!" gasped Miss Slade as she took off the last of the wrapping. "I haven't had a camera since I had a box Brownie when I was Patsy's age. How wonderful! How absolutely lovely! Show me how it works, Robert, and I'll take a picture of you all."

"We must have one of you, too, Maggie," said Susan, "in your finery."

Before it gets too filthy, she thought.

So before she left to go home, Miss Slade put on her red field jacket and her red gloves and her green scarf and her red hat with earflaps, and posed for her picture between Moke, who had eaten his carrots, string bag and all, and Edward, who had reduced his marrow bone to a small wreck.

Back at Blackberry Bottom, she fed her hens and picked up their eggs, fed her goats and milked them, fed her six cats and her six dogs, and took photos of every one of them.

That evening, sitting in the old caravan with the dogs, she thought, What a lovely birthday it has been.

She looked at Jim's picture of Moke, which was pinned on the wall with Patsy's poem beside it. She read the last couplet:

*And the special lady is our friend*
*And she is called Miss Slade.*

*The End*

Tiddler began yapping as usual, meaning, "Tell us about your day."

"All right," said Miss Slade. "But first I must tell you that before long, possibly even in time for Christmas, we shall not be sitting here together anymore. We shall be sitting in a great big brand-new caravan. But whether it's ready in time or not, this Christmas I shall not be alone. Not that I'm ever really alone as long as I've got you, my dears. But now at long last I have made some good friends: Robert, who will look after my money matters; Susan, who will look after getting me new clothes and stuff; and Patsy and Jim, who think that I'm special."

Miss Slade looked at the six different faces upturned to hers, and with her one eye she saw the devotion shining out of their twelve eyes.

"Do *you* think I'm special?" she said, and in answer they all suddenly burst out barking.

# ABOUT THE AUTHOR

Dick King-Smith was born and raised in Gloucestershire, England. He served in the Grenadier Guards during World War II, then returned home to Gloucestershire to realize his lifelong ambition of farming. After twenty years as a farmer, he turned to teaching and then to writing the children's books that have earned him many fans on both sides of the Atlantic. Inspiration for his writing has come from his farm and his animals.

Among his well-loved novels for younger readers are *Babe: The Gallant Pig, Three Terrible Trins, Harriet's Hare,* and *A Mouse Called Wolf.* In 1992, he was named Children's Author of the Year at the British Book Awards. In 1995, *Babe: The Gallant Pig* was made into a critically acclaimed major motion picture that was later nominated for an Academy Award.